VENOM ADVENTURES

MARVEL ADVENTURES SPIDER-MAN #21

Writer: **Fred Van Lente**
Penciler: **Michael O'Hare**
Inker: **Cory Hamscher**
Colorist: **Guru-eFX**
Letterer: **Dave Sharpe**
Cover Art: **Patrick Scherberger, Roland Paris & Guru-eFX**
Assistant Editor: **Nathan Cosby**
Editor: **Mark Paniccia**

MARVEL ADVENTURES SPIDER-MAN #24

Writer: **Fred Van Lente**
Artist: **Cory Hamscher**
Colorist: **Guru-eFX**
Letterer: **Dave Sharpe**
Cover Art: **Patrick Scherberger, Roland Paris & Guru-eFX**
Assistant Editor: **Nathan Cosby**
Editor: **Mark Paniccia**

MARVEL ADVENTURES SPIDER-MAN #35

Writer: **Fred Van Lente**
Artists: **Cory Hamscher** with **Terry Pallot**
Colorist: **Guru-eFX**
Letterer: **Dave Sharpe**
Cover Art: **Patrick Scherberger, Roland Paris & Guru-eFX**
Assistant Editor: **Nathan Cosby**
Editor: **Mark Paniccia**

MARVEL UNIVERSE ULTIMATE SPIDER-MAN #16

Based on "Back in Black" by Man of Action

Adapted by **Joe Caramagna**
Cover Art: **Ty Templeton**
Editor: **Sebastian Girner**
Senior Editor: **Mark Paniccia**

MARVEL UNIVERSE ULTIMATE SPIDER-MAN #19

Based on "Venomous" by Man of Action

Adapted by **Joe Caramagna**
Cover Art: **Ty Templeton**
Editor: **Sebastian Girner**
Senior Editor: **Mark Paniccia**

Collection Editor: **Jennifer Grünwald**
Assistant Editor: **Caitlin O'Connell**
Associate Managing Editor: **Kateri Woody**
Editor, Special Projects: **Mark D. Beazley**

VP Production & Special Projects: **Jeff Youngquist**
SVP Print, Sales & Marketing: **David Gabriel**
Research: **Jess Harold**
Book Designer: **Adam Del Re**

Editor in Chief: **C.B. Cebulski**
Chief Creative Officer: **Joe Quesada**
President: **Dan Buckley**
Executive Producer: **Alan Fine**

VENOM ADVENTURES. Contains material originally published in magazine form as MARVEL ADVENTURES SPIDER-MAN #21, #24 and #35; and MARVEL UNIVERSE ULTIMATE SPIDER-MAN #16 and #19. First printing 2018. ISBN 978-1-302-91363-2. Published by MARVEL WORLDWIDE, INC., a subsidiary of MARVEL ENTERTAINMENT, LLC. OFFICE OF PUBLICATION: 135 West 50th Street, New York, NY 10020. Copyright © 2018 MARVEL No similarity between any of the names, characters, persons, and/or institutions in this magazine with those of any living or dead person or institution is intended, and any such similarity which may exist is purely coincidental. **Printed in the U.S.A.** DAN BUCKLEY, President, Marvel Entertainment; JOHN NEE, Publisher; JOE QUESADA, Chief Creative Officer; TOM BREVOORT, SVP of Publishing; DAVID BOGART, SVP of Business Affairs & Operations, Publishing & Partnership; DAVID GABRIEL, SVP of Sales & Marketing, Publishing; JEFF YOUNGQUIST, VP of Production & Special Projects; DAN CARR, Executive Director of Publishing Technology; ALEX MORALES, Director of Publishing Operations; DAN EDINGTON, Managing Editor; SUSAN CRESPI, Production Manager; STAN LEE, Chairman Emeritus. For information regarding advertising in Marvel Comics or on Marvel.com, please contact Vit DeBellis, Custom Solutions & Integrated Advertising Manager, at vdebellis@marvel.com. For Marvel subscription inquiries, please call 888-511-5480. **Manufactured between 7/20/2018 and 8/21/2018 by SHERIDAN, CHELSEA, MI, USA.**

10 9 8 7 6 5 4 3 2 1

MARVEL ADVENTURES SPIDER-MAN #21

BITTEN BY AN IRRADIATED SPIDER, WHICH GRANTED HIM INCREDIBLE ABILITIES, PETER PARKER LEARNED THE ALL-IMPORTANT LESSON, THAT WITH GREAT POWER THERE MUST ALSO COME GREAT RESPONSIBILITY. AND SO HE BECAME THE AMAZING SPIDER-MAN
Y-y-you just stay b-b-back, S-S-Spider-Man!
I-I-I don't wanna hurt you!
Awwww. A crook who cares. I'm touched!
But since you're clearly new at this, let me give a piece of free advice, Tony Hawk...
BANK OF
Fashion Victims!
FRED VAN LENTE WRITER
MICHAEL O'HARE PENCILS
CORY HAMSCHER INKS
GURU eFX COLORS
SCHERBERGER, PARIS and GURU eFX COVER
DAVE SHARPE LETTERER
KATE LEVIN PRODUCTION
NATHAN COSBY ASST. EDITOR
MARK PANICCIA EDITOR
JOE QUESADA CHIEF
DAN BUCKLEY PUBLISHER

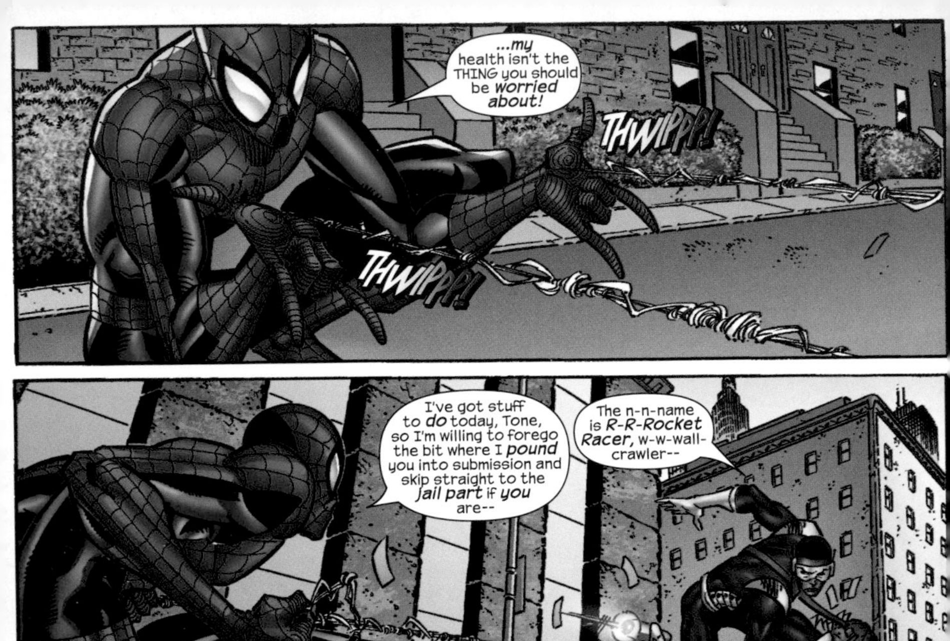
...my health isn't the THING you should be worried about!
THWIPPP!
THWIPPP!

I've got stuff to do today, Tone, so I'm willing to forego the bit where I pound you into submission and skip straight to the jail part if you are--
The n-n-name is R-R-Rocket Racer, w-w-wall-crawler--

POW!!
POW!!
POW!!
--for r-r-reasons that should be obvious even to somebody with your l-l-limited cranial capacity!

"Limited cranial capacity?"
WHOOOOA!
BAMM!
BAMM!

KRASH!
Well, lookee here!
You sure got a lotta muscles on you for a little guy!
Ohhhh... Aunt May?
What's this?
One of Rocket Raccoon's mini-missiles must have been a dud!
Huh! Some kind of maker's mark. Must be a clue...
...though to what I haven't got a...
...uh, clue.
Drivers are advised to avoid Park Avenue above Grand Central due to a robbery in progress by a man in a super-suit--
Must be that skateboarding guy again! He does get around fast...

Sure you won't stick around, squirt? I'd love for you to show me what's under that mask--
Gulp! No thanks, lady!
I'm afraid you'd show me what's under yours!

Your jewels couldn't be in a more secure location, Mrs. Gilcrest, sixty floors above street level...
But then your security system can hardly be blamed...
...for there's not a burglar alarm on Earth that could protect you from...
...the stupendous Stilt-Man! Ha, ha, ha, ha!!!
Tsk! Y'see? That's the problem with conventional wisdom, my friend...
...it's so often totally wrong! Haw!
No!! Stop him--

TRIP!
WHOAA... WHOOOOAAAA...
AAAAAHHHH!
How you gonna stop that nutjob, Spidey?!
Well...to thwart a menace of this magnitude requires a very sophisticated and specialized crime-fighting technique...
CRASH!
Oh. You were being sarcastic.
Yes. Yes, I was.

Okay. So you're not the skateboarding guy.
What is this, "Better Thieving Through Technology" Day?
Grooooooan
All right... this officially constitutes a pattern...
You stay away from my buddy Stilt-Man, Mr. Bug...
SLAMMMM!
UNNNNH!
...or you'll face the lacerating leaps of the larcenous Leap-Frog!
BOING!
BOING!

That's a risk I'm willing to take.
ZWOK!
MIA'S CAFE

Now, where was I? Oh, yeah. Listen up, tall guy--
Stilt-Man!
Whatever!

You gonna tell me where all you technologically-enhanced freaks are coming from of your own free will...

...or am I gonna have to use harsh language?

SPRONG!

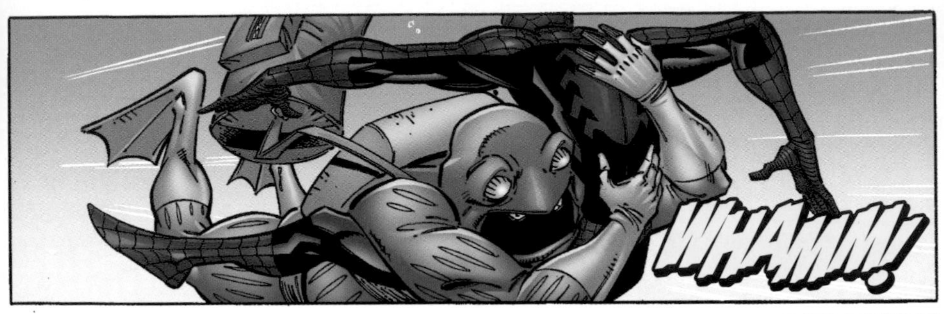
WHAMM!

KKRUNCHH!

Wilbur! pant! Help! I'm stuck! gasp!
And I left my inhaler back at the hideout! pant!
Don't use my real name, Eugene! Chill and put your trust in your partner in crime...

...'cause Stilt-Man controls the horizontal as well as the vertical!
Heh. Outer Limits reference. Good one, Wilbur.

C'mon! Let's go see if Bob was as successful at his crimes as we were!
Hello! A little help!
The Jaws of Life, anyone?

Between the c-c-cash I got at the bank...the jewels W-W-Wilbur nabbed and the savings bonds Eugene, a-a-acquired, ha-ha...

...well, let's just s-s-say there won't be a piece of a new t-t-tech to come out in the better part of a year that we won't be able to a-a-afford!
Awesome! I'm gonna get a Y-Box game console--the one that jacks directly into your brain!
I'm headed straight to Electrono-Mart for that plasma screen TV that's so big it can be seen from space!

The "Big T" is gonna be so proud of us! I hope he doesn't ask for his gear back!
I could get used to a life of cri...
Hey...

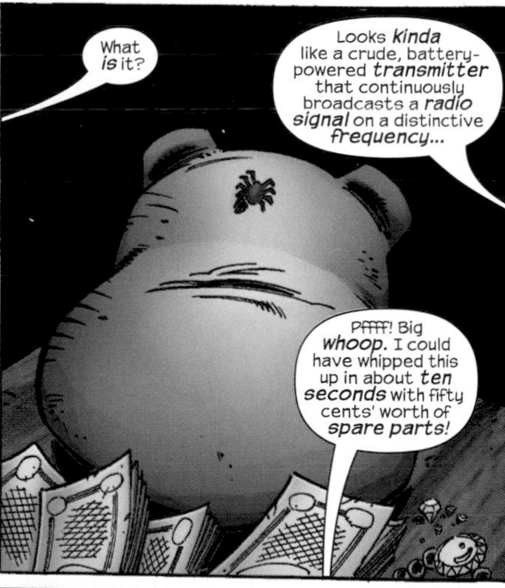
What is it?
Looks kinda like a crude, battery-powered transmitter that continuously broadcasts a radio signal on a distinctive frequency...
Pffff! Big whoop. I could have whipped this up in about ten seconds with fifty cents' worth of spare parts!

Everybody's a critic!

I know my spider tracers don't look like much, but they get the job done.

Oh no, you don't.
We're not going through all that again.
THWIP!
THWIP!

Muuuuuuch better.
So who's this "Big T" who will be so proud of you? He the mastermind behind your little crime spree?

As if! Unlike you, we don't need any extra brain power! "Big T" basically works for us!
W-W-Wilbur! Sshhhh!!
You shush, Bob! If we don't school our mental inferiors, how will they ever better themselves?
"We three met online at a message board for connoisseurs of the mechanical arts.
"One of the other posters was this guy we knew only by his screen name...
"...'Tinkerer.'
GADGET SHACK 200
"Well, we got to complaining about how we were strapped for cash, and couldn't afford all the new gadgets as they came onto the market..."
W-w-why should we?
Well...I know a certain friendly neighborhood Spider-Man who's been shopping for some costume enhancements lately...
...and he's willing to pay top dollar for 'em!
But he'd settle for putting "Big T" out of business-- permanently!
...so, out of the blue, Tinkerer offered us these awesome super-suits for free, no strings attached!
Wow. Now that's what I call a real pal.
Think you could arrange a meet between your mysterious benefactor and me?
I'm sick of fighting crooks that are dorkier than I am!

Now boys ⁻heh!⁻, I thought we agreed we'd keep our little ⁻heh!⁻ arrangement just between us techies...
It's cool, Mr. T, we'll vouch for him!
H-h-he was so impressed with how y-y-your inventions were used against him, h-h-he wanted some for himself!
But ⁻heh!⁻, Spider-Man on the side of criminality? I find that just a wee bit ⁻heh!⁻ implausible...
Hardly... lookee here--
"2100% increase in NYC crime since Spider-Man appeared"..."Spider-Man causes twenty-five-car pileup on Brooklyn-Queens Expressway"..."Sources: Spider-Man has poor personal hygiene..."
If you can't trust the first name in journalism, J. Jonah Jameson of the Daily Bugle, who can you trust?
DAILY
SPIDER MENACE!
All right... these appear to be in order...
...let me get your paperwork started...

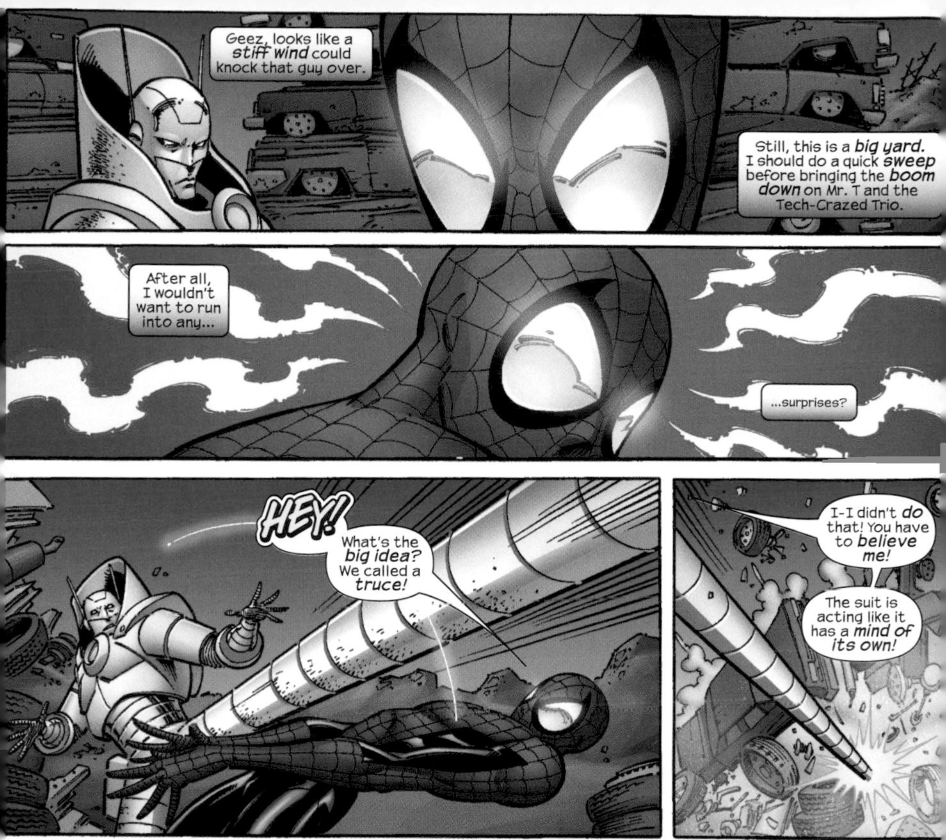

Geez, looks like a stiff wind could knock that guy over.
Still, this is a big yard. I should do a quick sweep before bringing the boom down on Mr. T and the Tech-Crazed Trio.
After all, I wouldn't want to run into any...
...surprises?
HEY!
What's the big idea? We called a truce!
I-I didn't do that! You have to believe me!
The suit is acting like it has a mind of its own!

U-u-us too! W-w-we're not in control of our own g-g-gadgets anymore!
K-POW!
UGH!
What's happening?!

HA HA HA HA HA!
You see, gentle-men? If the Tinkerer's technology can turn these three -heh!- pitiable nerds into unstoppable super-villains...
...imagine what my devices could do for your hardened gangsters!
My original product demonstration was going to consist solely of my -heh!- protegés' daring daylight robberies.
But now, under my remote control, I shall prove, beyond a shadow of a doubt, my super-suit's efficacy...
...by destroying Spider-Man!
The exclusive contract for my services begins at -heh!- five million dollars!
Six million!
Ten!

Pardon me.
Ow!
S-s-sorry.
Ow!
Didn't mean it!
Ow!
I gotta get out of here--regroup! Come up with a strategy!
Where are you going? You have to save us!
Save you? Who's gonna save me?
FFFSSSSss
Oh, great! I knew I should have refilled my web shooters before adhering those bozos to the wall...
I h-h-hope you w-w-won't hold our actions tonight a-a-against us.
WHUDDD!

This hurts us more than it hurts you!
WOK!

Y-yeow--
That I sincerely doubt!

Cut it out, Bob! You're more than my gyro-stabilizers can handle--
SLAMM!

Whoaaa-- not again--
Look, guys! He's very erratically getting away!
CRASSSH!

C-can't h-hold on m-much l-longer--

YAAHHHH!

Whoof!
That spider-agility does come in mighty handy.

But I'll need more than that to get me out of this mess--
--I could use some kind of edge, especially since my web-shooters are empty!

Looks like I've stumbled across one of the Tinkerer's laboratories. Maybe I'll be able to find an invention that can help me.
"Smart stealth cloth," huh? I guess some kind of camouflage could be useful.
SMART STEALTH CLOTH

But this doesn't look like any kind of fabric I've ever seen.
Almost more of a liquid metal, like mercury--
SMART STEALTH CLOTH

HELLO!
It's--crawling across my body--almost like it was alive!
!!!
Incredible! It must have sensed that I wanted some kind of camouflage--read my surface thoughts!
If that doesn't put the "smart" in "smart stealth cloth", I don't know what does!
'Cause all on its lonesome, it decided to create for me a brand-new costume!!

Gentlemen... our prey is cornered.
That means we near -heh!- endgame.
One hundred million dollars!
One million ten!

I-I-I don't know if I c-c-can watch me do th-th-this!
Spidey doesn't stand a chance!

Let's just hope his end is quick and relatively painless!
KRASH!

B-b-but...I didn't see him l-l-leave, did y-y-you?
Of course not!

I bet you he's hiding under one of those work-benches over there!

If it's possible to fall in *love* with a pair of *long underwear*, then I'm *head over heels.*
I just *think* about shooting out webbing, and the smart cloth *forms some* out of its own substance!
Thank you, Flash Thompson, for tying my *shoelaces* together in *geometry* last week, thereby giving me the *idea* for this...
Hey! *Tinkerer!*
Don't just *do* something!
Stand there!

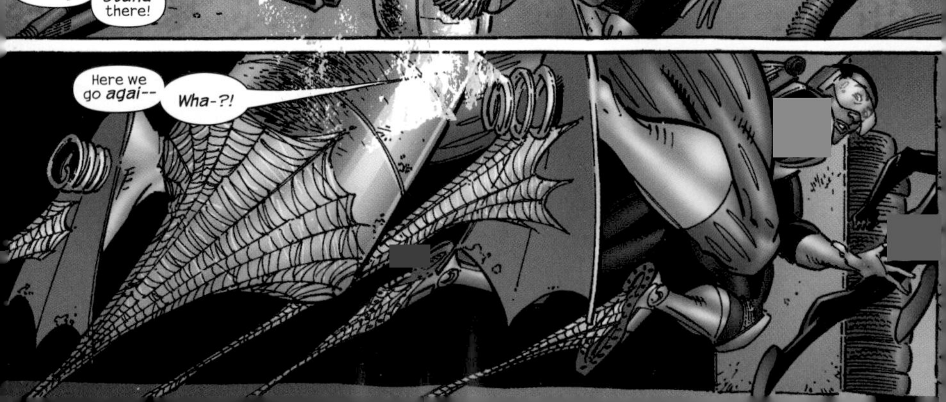
Here we go *agai--*
Wha-?!

CRASH!
You look to be way beyond retirement age, Pops...
...and I'm here to deliver your gold watch!
No!! Where--where are my cat's-paws?!
Oooohhhh...
Is that--my smart stealth cloth you're wearing?
Hey, imitation is the sincerest form of me kicking your tail, Tink.

Do I hear any objections from the peanut gallery?
Uh-- signing off!
You have failed, Tinkerer. My organization shall take its business elsewhere.
Gotta say you have exactly zero reason to look so pleased with your-self, Pops.
I'm afraid -heh!- store policy is that damaged merchandise is non-returnable, Spider-Man...
...particularly after the -heh!- warranty has expired.
Say, what now?
YOWZA!
BBBBZZZZT!
Now there's something you don't see every day.
Either the Tinkerer was, himself, a machine...
...or that was a robot replica, and the real Tinkerer is halfway to Poughkeepsie by now!
Still, if this caper accomplished nothing else, I got some spiffy new threads out of it...
...even Spider-Man ...ld ...e a di... outfit to ...nge into every once in a while!
The End

MARVEL ADVENTURES SPIDER-MAN #24

TEENAGER PETER PARKER WAS BITTEN BY AN IRRADIATED SPIDER WHICH GRANTED HIM INCREDIBLE ABILITIES -- ABILITIES THAT ARE NOW ENHANCED BY A HIGH-TECH "SMART STEALTH" BLACK COSTUME TAKEN FROM A VILLAIN THAT ALLOWS HIM TO CREATE "NATURAL" WEBBING AND TURN INSTANTLY INTO THE AMAZING SPIDER-MAN
'Sup.
YAAAAAAH!
I'm bad with traffic laws...
...which one of us has the right-of-way?
BREAKING UP IS VENOMOUS TO DO!
FRED VAN LENTE WRITER
CORY HAMSCHER ARTIST
GURU eFX COLORISTS
DAVE SHARPE LETTERER
SCHERBERGER, HAMSCHER et GURU eFX COVER
DAVE SHARPE PRODUCTION
NATHAN COSBY ASSISTANT EDITOR
MARK PANICCIA EDITOR
JOE QUESADA EDITOR IN CHIEF
DAN BUCKLEY PUBLISHER

Hey, buddy, don't blame me. There'd be a lot less congestion up here...
...if you could learn to keep... your sticky fingers...
...to... yourself... ohhhh...
No! Look what you made me do!
It took me months to plan this job!
Whoa!
?!?
Whoa!
WHOA!
SQUELLLLLLL
How embarrassing.
And potentially crippling!

THWIP!
THUD!
Ugh! Not only have I lost my ability to stick to walls...
...my head feels like it's been run over by a Mack truck.
Repeatedly and with extreme prejudice!
What's happening to me? Just the other night, I got so winded I let an entire gang of crooks get away!
It's not like I don't get enough regular exercise...and during the day, when I'm Peter Parker, I feel fine!
There's gotta be something wrong with my superhuman physiology...and it's not like I can just drop by Dr. Goplan's on Roosevelt Avenue for a checkup on that!
No, I need somebody qualified to examine super-types and not ask too many questions while doing it...
...so that narrows my choices down to exactly one guy:

A scientist who's a super hero himself...Dr. Reed Richards of the
FANTASTIC FOUR!
I knew you'd finally crack up, Wall-Crawler!
But you do know psychiatry happens to be one of the few sciences Reed doesn't have a Ph.D. in?
If I'd known you were going to be here too, Torch, I would've scheduled an appointment with Dr. Doom!

Hmmm...though all my instruments appear properly calibrated...
...they're picking up two life readings off you, Spider-Man! How can that be accurate?
Unless...

...this new costume you're wearing. You say it's made of a "smart stealth" material that can read your surface thoughts--move on and off of you under its own power--and form "natural webbing" out of itself?
Yeah! It's the greatest!
Hmmm... that may very well be...

...but that costume is technology, and all technology requires a power source.
My sensors suggest the costume is siphoning off your body's own bioelectrical energy in order to fuel itself!
That would explain why you've been feeling so weak and winded lately...

...and why you've lost your ability to stick to walls.
Just like insects and spiders, microscopic hairs on your hands and feet adhere on the molecular level to exterior surfaces--super static cling, if you will.
Any reduction in bioelectricity will weaken that bond.
I can't be sure until I run further tests, though.
So I'm going to have to ask you to leave your costume here.
Er...all right... but, uh...not that I don't trust you, Doc...
...but I'll need something to conceal my secret identity... particularly while I'm heading home!
I've got just the thing, Reed!
That's very considerate of you, Johnny.
You never looked better, Web-Head!
Yeah...thanks for nothin', Matchstick...
HUMAN TORCH RULES !!!

Later that night, in Fantastic Four Headquarters...

Heh, heh!
The perfect crime!

"Maybe the Wall-Crawler can't handle this super-suit...

"...but I would look so sweet in black I can barely stand it!"

SWISSH!
I'm sure Reed won't mind me just trying it on...

Gross!
It's...like... tingly!

Wow! It really can read my surface thoughts!
Let's see if it looks as cool after I...
...flame on!
FWOOOOSH!
Oops.
Forgot I wasn't wearing my unstable molecule pajamas.
Oh, no!
Looks like I burned up the black costume, too!
I don't see it anywhere!

Blast that Spider-Man!
He made me lose a year's worth of hard work!
If I ever see that meddling so-and-so again--

Yuck!
What kind of oil slick sticks to the wall of a building--?
Aaaaaggh! It's moving-- like it's alive!
Get it off me!

Wha--
Images--flooding into my brain--
Saying--I can shoot webs? Out of my hands?
THWIPP!
Hey--that's no lie!
I don't believe it! This crazy material is--communicating with me, inside my head!
What's that, now? You want to find Spider-Man? Hey, me too!
His real name is--Peter Parker--and he's some punk kid--living in Queens?
Well, what are we hanging around here for?
We're wasting precious revenge time!

Awwww, look at him--
--the snot-nosed brat!
I can feel you wanting to go in there right now, buddy.
Now I feel the same way as you do--
--but taking him out now would be far too easy! Particularly since we know every-thing about him:
Where he goes to school--what Aunt May's favorite dish to cook for him is--
We should use that knowledge to take him out in the cruelest way possible!
HA HA HA
HA HA HA HA HA
?

The following morning...

Oh...
Real mature, Flash!

What'd you do with my clothes?
Pfff! Please! What do I want with your hand-me-downs?
My mom's already got all the dishrags she needs!

Nice one, dude! How'd you swipe Puny Parker's civvies out of his locker with the lock still on?
I didn't! You mean that wasn't you that took them...?

I don't believe this...

Looking for these?
Wha-?
HOW?!
Oh--you'll need your web shooters too, Parker! You don't have any "natural" webbing any more, after all...
Who... who are you?
We are two, who you are meeting again for the first time.
One of us is Eddie Brock, a hard-working burglar, whose heist you ruined...
...the other, a loyal companion who you threw aside as soon as you lost interest in him!
Together, however, we are double what we were without the other-- and our disdain for you is twice as strong!
Call us... VENOM.

Our beef is with Spider-Man, Parker. Don your true, traitorous colors...
...so we can destroy you in them!
Er...can't we talk about this first?
Like--what if I wore black on alternating Tuesdays?
You have the gall to make jokes?
After wrecking our lives?!
Oof!
Hey, c'mon now--
--don't you think "wrecking" is just a wee bit melodramat--
UNK!
KRRAAKKK!

Who asked you to butt in in the first place?
You're no cop! You're getting what you deserve for sticking your nose into other people's business--
THWIPP!
FWOOSH!
YAAAAHHH!
That water-- it's scalding hot!
Wait-- where are you going?
We almost have him!

Hmmm... psycho costume doesn't like heat. Good to know.
Come back here!

'Afternoon, ladies!
Who's winning?

Ahhh... Liz Allen, right?
You're just as pretty as Spider-Man remembers you!

How-- how does that thing know my name?!
How does Spider-Man?
I'M TOTALLY FREAKING OUT HERE!

We could have used a different name for you back there--one that rhymes with "Marker!"
But we
GO TIGERS!!
Good for you! Your medal's in the mail!
One for both of you!
Not so fast! We know what you're trying to do--lure us out of the school to keep your classmates from danger
But that's not going to happen!
THWAPP!
LIBRA
We will crush you in front of them--then unmask you, making your humiliation that much sweeter!
So we choose not to reveal your identity until then!
Not that I'm saying that that plan isn't completely awesome--because it so totally is--
EXIT
--but my doctor said getting crushed was absolutely, positively the worst thing for me!

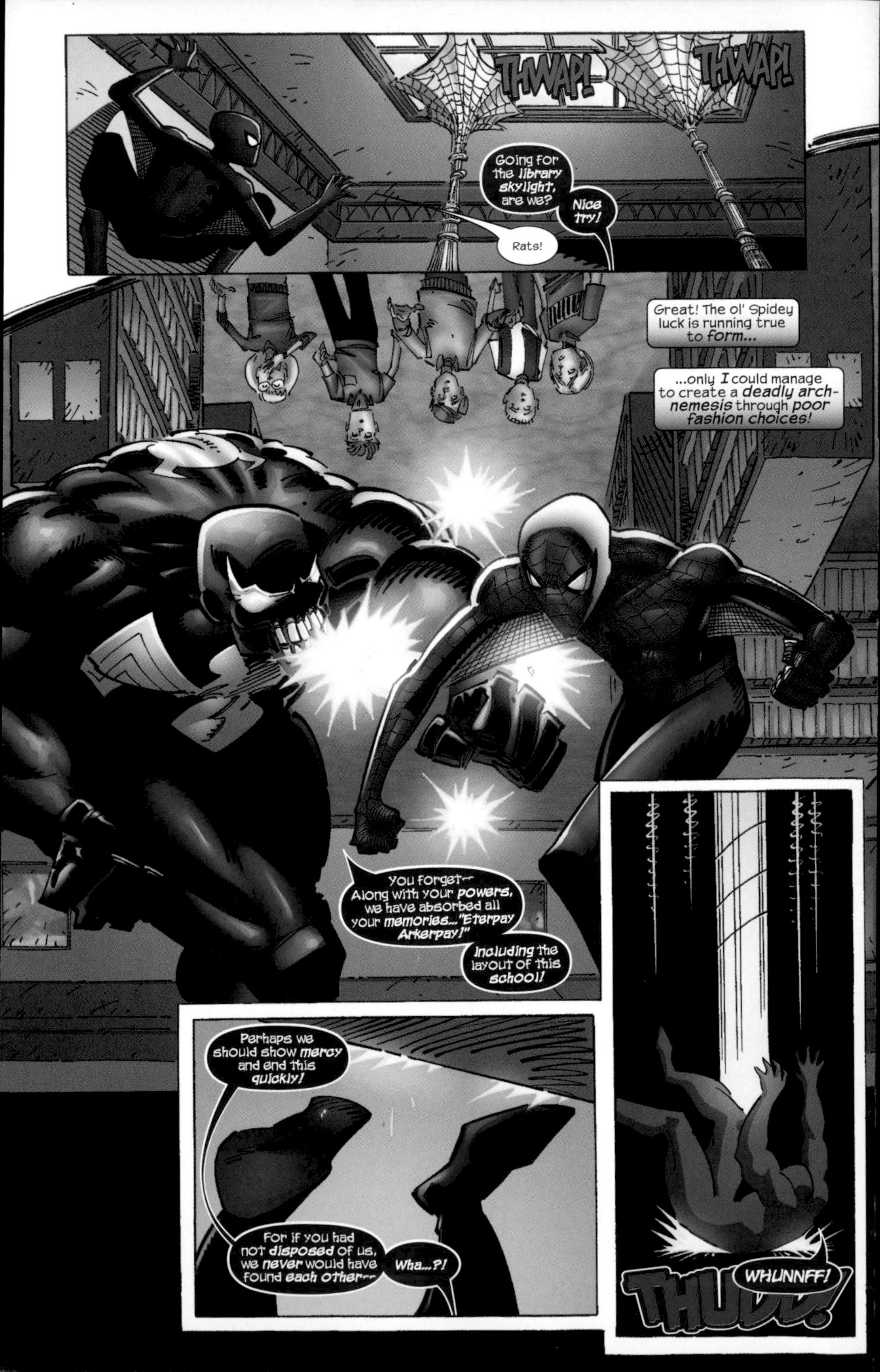
THWAP! THWAP!
Going for the library skylight, are we?
Nice try!
Rats!
Great! The ol' Spidey luck is running true to form...
...only I could manage to create a deadly arch-nemesis through poor fashion choices!
You forget-- Along with your powers, we have absorbed all your memories..."Eterpay Arkerpay!"
Including the layout of this school!
Perhaps we should show mercy and end this quickly!
For if you had not disposed of us, we never would have found each other--
Wha...?!
WHUNNFF!
THUDD!

What happened...?
I bet I know!
Brock's not super-powered like me! The outfit is going to burn through his "normal" level of bioelectric energy that much more rapidly!
What I want to know is...
...is the smart costume smart enough to figure that out too?
CHEM. LAB
Feeling... a little...out of sorts...
But I still have plenty of strength left to finish you!
Oh, yeah, your tank's still almost full, Venom-baby!
See? You managed to knock me all the way back into this here chemistry lab!

We will knock you into next week!
Once you stop... moving around... from side to side... like that...
Wait just a second, Venom! I have to admit--all your speechifying has been pretty persuasive.
With all its cool bonus features, I was a total bonehead to get rid of my black costume!
Can you hear me, pal? I've learned my lesson--I was wrong, and I'm sorry. I'd love to have you back...
...if you can forgive me, that is!
Ha! Your crocodile tears come too little, too late, Spider-Man!
We are united in our all-consuming hatred for you and no amount of begging can stave off your imminent destruc--

Wait--where are you going?!
We're a team--two minds working toward a single purpose--
Don't--don't leave me!

Ouch. I feel for you, Brockster.
It stinks to be the rebound host.

That's right, come to Papa.
I'm just a moveable feast to you, aren't I? One all-you-can-eat proportionate-strength-of-a-spider bioelectric buffet...
Psyche!
THWIP!
THWIP!
CRASH!
Stop! What are you doing?!
C'mon, Eddie...
...what's a little chemical fire between friends?

You should have stayed with *me*!
Only *I* truly *understood* you!

Au contraire, Edward.
The hatred you projected onto the costume was all your *own*--it was just using *you* to get close to a better *power source*!
BONK!

Mrs. Aguilera, my science teacher, is gonna have a cow when she sees this!
At least I'll be able to keep her *teachers' editions* from going up in flames!
SSSSSHHHHH

Hey...is that the cat burglar--Eddie Brock?
There are APBs out on him from *five precincts*!

Wait--wait--I got something to--I gotta tell you--and the *world*!
The secret of the *century*!
The Wall-Crawler's *secret identity*!

He's really--
--uh--
--really--
I--I don't remember!
The memories I got off the suit are gone--along with the power!
Suuuuure, Eddie.
Don't worry--we're fittin' you for a new orange suit that's got special powers too!
Prison powers!
Oh, well. It stinks I had to give up my black costume, but it does feel good to be back in the ol' red-and-blues again.
Guess it's true, what they say about fashion:
EXIT
One day you're in ...
...the next day, you're out!
The End...?

MARVEL ADVENTURES SPIDER-MAN #35

BITTEN BY AN IRRADIATED SPIDER, WHICH GRANTED HIM INCREDIBLE ABILITIES, PETER PARKER LEARNED THE ALL-IMPORTANT LESSON, THAT WITH GREAT POWER THERE MUST ALSO COME GREAT RESPONSIBILITY. AND SO HE BECAME THE AMAZING
SPIDER-MAN
Help! HELLLLP!
I'm being mugged!
The SIDE-KICK
FRED VAN LENTE WRITER
CORY HAMSCHER WITH TERRY PALLOT ART
GURU eFX COLORS
DAVE SHARPE LETTERS
FRANCIS TSAI COVER
ANTHONY DIAL PRODUCTION
NATHAN COSBY ASST. EDITOR
MARK PANICCIA EDITOR
JOE QUESADA EDITOR IN CHIEF
DAN BUCKLEY PUBLISHER

Th-thank you for stopping! I'm a very rich man! I own the Maple Log Molasses company!
I'll pay whatever you want! Just keep those crazies away from me!
Lucky for you, Pops, I'm crazy enough to do this stuff for free.
Although... if I have to fight crooks this dumb-looking...
...how much is it worth to you, exactly?
OFF WIT' HIS HEAD!
So many wisecracks... leaping into my mind...all at once...causing... brain aneurysm...
Don't know where to begin...
Wait! Wait! I know!
Time to cut the cards...
...with extreme prejudice!

No, that's *lame.* How about:
I'm gonna *fold* this hand faster than *Superguy* on *laundry day!*
AAAAAAAAAAGGGH!
Aw, c'mon. It wasn't that bad.
The problem is I have *too much* material to work with here...

Spider-Man...
GAAGH!
Ah. Our apologies. We forget we are invisible to your spider-sense because half of us is the "smart stealth" costume you once wore.
No! We're trying to help you against them!
Yeah, right. You expect me to believe that?
Venom! You're with the 52 Pickup Gang?
I've heard of not playing with a full deck, but this is ridiculous!
Heh. You still got it, Spidey.
Not without proof!
LOOK!

S-scary m-m-monster...
K-keep him a-a-away...
"But we used the stealth technology in your old suit to sneak up on him!"
hat one as gonna ushwhack you from th alley!
Yeah? Last time we met, you were trying to pop my head off.
What's with the chummy-chummy act?
S-Spider-M-Man... h-help me...
We had a lot of time to think during our last stint in prison.

"Or at least the human half of us, Eddie Brock, did.
"The warden kept the sentient costume part of us in line by bombarding it with sonics, its one true weakness."
We're sick of being hounded by the law! We want to use our powers to help people, just like you!
Show us the ropes, Spider-Man! Let us apprentice ourselves to you...as your sidekick!
They'll call us "Venom...Lethal Protector!"

What? That could be the worst idea I ever heard... and my whole life has been one bad idea after another!
Forget it! No way I'm going to let a psycho like you be my shadow!
You shouldn't dismiss us so easily, Web-head!
Remember-- this costume absorbed all your memories while you wore it...so we know all that you know!
We'll tell the whole world your real name is Peter Parker!
Fine. Go ahead. Maybe I should have done it a long time ago.
We'll tell Aunt May where you have your massive candy stash hidden in your closet!
No...not my Pixie Stix!!
And we'll tell Liz Allen who slipped those secret admirer notes into her locker freshman year!!
NO! WAIT!
Okay, you win. I'll let you tag along on my regular patrol-- tonight only--but I decide whether or not you get to be my "sidekick" permanently...
...and my decision will be final! You got that?
Whatever you say, S.M.!
And don't call me S.M.

So most nights this job is nowhere near as exciting as they make it out to be in the comics.
I just swing my usual route, check in on the usual trouble spots...
...Central Park...
...Rockefeller Center...
...Empire State.

But the night's highlight is always here, at Fifty-third and Ninth!
Yeah? Some kind of underworld hangout?
No, no, no. Much better.
Free pizza!
FAMOUS RAY'S FAMOUSER PIZZA
RAY'S
Hey, Spidey! What's the good word?
You bring a friend tonight?
Yeah, can I get an extra slice, Ray?
You got it! Anything for my friendly neighbor-hood wall-crawler!
I saved Ray's from getting trashed by the Rhino last fall.
Slurp! I heard that guy's got no class.
So this is all you do every night? Swing past a bunch of darkened buildings and eat pizza?
On the good nights, sure. I imagine it's hard for a guy like you to understand...
...but we're here to protect the peace. So we like it peaceful.

Bah! We can barely keep our eyes open!
There must be something happening at Times Square!
But that's not on our route for another forty-five minutes...
Oh, okay. Why not?
A-ha! Your spider-sense just go off too?
Yeah...
WOO-WOO! WOO-WOO! WOO-WOO! WOO-WOO!
We must be your lucky charm, webslinger!
We've led you right to some gen-yoo-whine criminal activities!

I'll go first, so you can see how it's done!
Sure...we're just the sidekick, and you're the main hero!
FZZZZZZ
Wha...my web-shooters--jammed!
But...I just reloaded them--
WHOOOOOOOAA--
Our webbing is a natural part of our costume itself! It never misfires!
So this looks like a job for Venom:
LETHAL PROTECTOR!!
Hold on! I got you, Spidey!
No, I can take care of myself!
Don't let those crooks get away!

THWAP!
There's a new spider hero in town, scum! And when we catch flies--
--we pull their wings o--
KRUNK!!
Whoop!

THUD!
KRONCH!
KRASSHHHH!!
Ooohhhh...
Somebody call 9-1-1...
Your crippling injuries and cries for mercy are no match for Venom...
...LETHAL PROTECTOR!!
Stop! Y-you got to r-read me my rights--
Your rights? All right-- we do requests:
You have the right to remain screaming.

AAAAAAAAHHH!
Start talking or I start seeing which parts of you are removable!
Venom! No! Don't hurt him!
Aw.
Why not?
Because I have enough problems with them as it is!
Freeze!
Squawrk! Attention! All available units! Report to the Morgan Library!
The rare manuscript collection has just been broken into! squawrk!
Hmmm...

This gang is dressed like the Mad Hatter, the March Hare and the Dormouse...
...all of whom attended the *Mad Tea Party* in Lewis Carroll's *Alice in Wonderland!*

That *mean* something to you?
Maybe... I'm seeing a *pattern* here.
Looks like these goofs just boosted solid silver *tea services* from *Northeby's Auction House,* down the block!

I *loved* Carroll as a kid... had all his books *memorized!*
Those *card nuts* earlier tonight were robbing a *molasses magnate.*
Another word for molasses is *"treacle"--that's* a major part of the Mad Tea Party, too!

On my *signal:*
One... *two...*
Holy *Themed Thieveries,* S.M.!

This *library robbery* could b part of the same *bookworm crime spree!*
e'd better vestigate! ethally!
Don't call me S.M.
OOF!

Yeesh... there's so much N.Y.P.D. down there, you'd think a donut factory exploded.
We'll get busted within half a second of showing our faces!
No problem-- not when we can instantly retract our "smart stealth costume" beneath our street clothes!
You have your Daily Bugle press pass? I can pass myself off as a reporter.
Yeah... how do you know I have a--
Oh. Right. Memories.
I'll be back as soon as I've drummed up some clues!
No--I'll come down to you, once I've taken off my spider mask...
And my spider shirt...
...and my...urk...
...spider booties...

Eventually...
If I'm lucky, I'll get there before Venom eats any of the witnesses...
Got it!
You... do?
That was quick!
Not really...I was gone twenty minutes.
Oh.
Anyway, I "interviewed" one of the library security guards.
You were right! The Wonderland Gang strikes again!
EXHIBIT
HALL 1
Cam 6
REC
"They overpowered the guards and made off with a rare 19th-century manuscript of that nursery rhyme, 'Twinkle, Twinkle, Little Star.'
"Witnesses saw their little rabbit car peeling off toward the West Side docks!"
Yeah, that fits their M.O.--The Mad Hatter sings 'Twinkle, Twinkle, Little Bat' during the tea party.
We need to get over to the docks right away! The cops are already headed over there!
Why let them have all the fun?
I'm right behind you! Just as soon as I get my... urk...
...spider booties on...

The police will be here any minute! How can you be sure this is the right boat?
Elementary, my dear Wacko:
S.S. DODGSON
Charles Dodgson was Lewis Carroll's real name!
S.S. DODGSON
Holy Literary Allusions! You're a genius, S.M.!
Seriously. Stop. Or I'll hit you.
Let's split up to search this tub! Whoever finds the baddies first, signals the other!
That's the first non-completely insane thing you've said all night.
You see? You're rubbing off on us!

?
Ah! There you are, Spider-Man!
Very punctual!
I do so hate to be late!
Especially when the hour is nigh for the ultimate triumph...
...of the
White Rabbit!

Your little sidekick, Venom, was early--
--I hate it when people are early!!! Makes everything so awkward!
I've read about his vulnerability to sound--so we strapped him to the ship's foghorn!
Surrender immediately, Wall-Crawler, or the Black Wonder gets blasted with 130 decibels!
Yeeeeahh... I'm not gonna surrender. So I guess you're just gonna have to blast him, huh?
You're tough but fair, Whitey!
What? Are you mocking me?
I'll do it! I'll horn him!
You're right, Webbed Crusader! No negotiating with super-villainy!
We deserve it! We were a bust... as your sidekick... and worse...
...as a lethal protector! Sob!

Oh, stop... just stop!! This is just nauseating!
Why... what do you mean?
How dumb do you think I am? When you were in the library, I checked my web-shooter cartridges, Venom!
"I saw you managed to switch the real ones with carts filled with your 'smart stealth' material!
"That's why my shooters jammed when you wanted them to!"
I just happened to wind up in spots tonight where I could've used a "smart costume's" powers of natural webbing--camouflage--instant removal!
You arranged this whole thing so I'd take the black costume back, didn't you?
B-but how could I have planned all those Lewis Carroll crimes?
Because I'm an expert on Carroll--
--and that makes you one too, because you have all my memories!!
You knew exactly when to go to Times Square for the high-speed chase--you instantly got the "clue" at the library that led us right here--
--but the real tip-off is that this scheme is so complicated and stupid--
--ONLY A SENTIENT COSTUME COULD HAVE COME UP WITH IT!!

It doesn't matter he's seen through our plan, Eddie darling!
As long as we have the Bushwick Deuces on our side, we still outnumber him 5-to-1!!
GET HIM, BOYS!!!
Uhhhh...
...no.
No? Really?
What if I said, "Get him, boys, please..."?
Look, lady, it's bad enough you pay us peanuts to dress up like playing cards and get beat up by super heroes.
But now we find out you're actually in league with that Venom psychopath?
Forget it! Me and my gang are goin' back to Brooklyn to boost hubcaps!
I don't need them, Eddie! I promised I'd do anything for you when I wrote you in prison...
...and I spent every last dime of my trust fund on super-weaponry!

THWAP!
THWAP!
THWIP!
THWIP!
Sigh.
Calling you a "Grade-Z loser villain"...
...would be an insult to the dignity of Grade-Z loser villains every-where...
You'd reject us twice? That's it! As soon as we get out of here, we're gonna--
Ngggggg!! YOU STUPID BIMBO!
You tied these bonds too tight! We can't break free--
Hey, do you see that? Rolling in from the sea?
What? No, I don't see any--
Fog. Definitely looks like fog.
FOGHORN
AROOOOOOOOGA!!
Arrrrgghh!!
Gotta say, Venom, old buddy, old pal, I don't think sidekicking is your bag...
...I see your future more in comic relief...
The End

MARVEL UNIVERSE ULTIMATE SPIDER-MAN #16

AAAAAHH!
SQUAWK!
WHAT IN THE--?
WEEOOO WEEOOO WEEOOO
FROOSH
--CALL FOR MORE BACKUP!
TELL THEM SOME DRAGON MAN ROBOT IS ON THE LOOSE IN MIDTOWN!

HERE I AM!
THE ONLY BACKUP YOU'LL NEED!
THWIP

FTT
WEB BALL IN THE CENTER POCKET!

KROOSH

BOOYAH!
CRUNCH

HE DID IT!
WAY TO GO!
FEAR NOT, NEW YORKERS--

SPIDER-MAN 2 IS ON THE JOB!
HUH?!

I TAKE ONE SICK DAY--
--AND I'VE ALREADY BEEN REPLACED!
"J. JONAH JAMESON OF DAILY BUGLE COMMUNICATIONS HERE..."

...TO ANNOUNCE THAT NEW YORK CITY FINALLY HAS A REAL SUPER HERO I CAN GET BEHIND!
SPIDER-MAN 2!

IT'S ABOUT TIME SOMEBODY DID IT RIGHT!
SPIDER-MAN 2 IS BIGGER, STRONGER AND FASTER THAN THAT OTHER WALL-CRAWLING MENACE--
AND UNLIKE THAT OTHER GUY, HE DOESN'T START MORE TROUBLE THAN HE STOPS!

I
INSTEAD OF RAISING SUSPICION BY PUTTING UP A WALL OF SECRECY, SPIDER-MAN 2 MAKES TIME FOR THE MEDIA--

rvelbook
BLACK SUIT SPIDEY
YOU HAVE
FRIENDS
Share:
Status
What's on your mind?
--AND HIS MILLIONS OF ADORING FANS!
Manhattan Girl
YOU'RE SO AWESOME!!!!
MARRY ME!!!!!!!!
Sunshine Sister
ME TOO!

IF I WERE THE MAYOR, I'D GIVE HIM A KEY TO THE CITY!
HECK, I'D ERECT A STATUE IN HIS HONOR! I MIGHT EVEN PAY FOR IT MYSELF!
NO, MISS BRANT, PUT DOWN MY CHECKBOOK!
STICK CLOSE, KID...
THE ALL-NEW ALL-DIFFERENT SPIDER-MAN

...AND HOPE THAT THE AWESOME IS CONTAGIOUS!
AHEM GOT A MINUTE TO CHAT?

PERHAPS YOU DON'T KNOW, BUT THE SPIDER MOTIF IS ALREADY TAKEN.
YOU'RE STILL BOTHERING TO SHOW UP?
STEP ASIDE, LAST SEASON'S MODEL!

WHAT'S GOT ME BOTHERED IS YOUR OUTFIT.
THE LAST TIME I SAW A GETUP LIKE THAT, IT MEANT TROUBLE.
YOU'RE NOT WHAT I THINK YOU ARE, ARE YOU?

THE ONLY THING I AM--
THWIP

--IS BETTER THAN YOU!
HEY!
I DIDN'T GET A CHANCE TO TRICK YOU INTO GIVING UP YOUR SECRET IDENTITY!

HUHN?
WHERE DID--?

LOOK OUT BELOW!
POUNCE!
GAH!
MY HEAD COLD MUST BE BLOCKING OUT MY SPIDER-SENSE!

LONG WAY DOWN, HUH?
OW. OW. OW. OW.
BUMP BUMP BUMP BUMP

ARE YOU SURE THAT'S THE **REAL** SPIDEY, ALEJANDRO?
I DUNNO, PABLO, BUT IF **I** WERE HIM I WOULDN'T **ADMIT** IT.
WHAT ABOUT YOU, JULIO?
D'YOU THINK HE'S GONNA **CRY?**
GEE, NOT TOO EMBARRASSING.

IS THAT HOW YOU WANT IT, MAN?
'CAUSE I CAN GIVE AS GOOD AS I--I--
AH-- AH--
AH-CHOO!
AWW, WHAT'S THE MATTER?
THE **BUG'S** CAUGHT A **BUG?**

HAVE FUN CLEANING OUT THE INSIDE OF YOUR MASK, BRO!
GET BACK HERE! I'M NOT DONE WITH--
AW, FORGET IT.

BET ON BLACK!
OUT WITH THE OLD AND IN WITH THE 2!
OH. I GET IT. 'CAUSE OF "SPIDER-MAN 2."
CLEVER.
SNF

MIDTOWN HIGH.
THE NEXT DAY.
YO, PETE! WAIT UP!

OH, HEY, HARRY!
UH... WOW.
WHAT?

YOU LOOK TERRIBLE. LIKE...REALLY BAD.
SOMETHING MUST BE GOING AROUND.
YEAH, I--HEY!
WHAT'S THAT?

ARE YOU WEARING BLING?

OH-- THAT'S WHAT I WANT TO TALK TO YOU ABOUT.

COME WITH ME TO THE BATHROOM!
THE WHERE?

WHAT GIVES, HARRY?
JUST MAKING SURE WE'RE ALONE.
I'VE GOT THE **BIGGEST SECRET** YOU'LL EVER HEAR IN YOUR ***LIFE!***

YOU KNOW THAT COOL, NEW HERO? THAT GUY IN THE BLACK SUIT?
SPIDER-MAN 2? I'VE HEARD OF HIM.
WELL...

...WATCH THIS!

HARRY!
Y-YOU'RE--

THAT'S RIGHT! ***I AM!***

N-NO...
Y-YOU'RE... Y-YOU'RE...

...VENOM!
NO!
I'M SPIDER-MAN 2!

COME ON, HARRY, TAKE THAT OFF!
P-PUT IT AWAY BEFORE SOMEBODY SEES IT!

Y-YOU CAN TAKE IT OFF, RIGHT?
OF COURSE I CAN!

ARE YOU FREAKED OUT?
I FREAKED YOU OUT.
YOUR BEST FRIEND IS THE BIGGEST STAR IN THE WORLD. THAT'S A LOT TO DIGEST.
BUT JUST WAIT UNTIL EVERYONE ELSE FINDS OUT! MY DAD WILL FINALLY BE PROUD OF ME!

AH, THAT EXPLAINS IT!
HARRY'S ALWAYS LOOKING FOR HIS FATHER'S APPROVAL, BUT "STORMIN' NORMAN" OSBORN DOESN'T ROLL THAT WAY.
Y'KNOW, I GOTTA ADMIT... THE WAY HE PUTS ON THAT BLACK COSTUME MUST MAKE LIFE SO MUCH EASIER.

D'OH!
RIP

WE BOTH KNOW THAT'S VENOM! THE SYMBIOTE SPIDER MONSTER THING THAT FOUGHT SPIDER-MAN!
JUST A SMALL PIECE OF IT.
BUT I'VE TOTALLY GOT IT TRAINED. I CAN CONTROL IT.
HARRY...
...BEING A SUPER HERO ISN'T EASY.
WITH GREAT POWER COMES GREAT RESPONSIBILITY, AND THAT THING--
I'M TELLING YOU, I HAVE IT UNDER CONTROL.

BUT WHAT HAPPENS IF YOU LOSE CONTROL?
I SSSSSAID...

...IT'S NOT A PROBLEM. I GOT IT WIRED IN.
I... I GOTTA GO.
HARRY, WAIT--!
DID YOU CATCH THAT? THAT "SSSS"?
NOT COOL.
"MY BEST FRIEND IS VENOM." IT SOUNDS LIKE THE NAME OF A BAD MADE-FOR-CABLE MOVIE-- AH...
...AHH...
AH-CHOO!

ICK! SORRY!
I GOTTA REMEMBER TO KEEP MY GERMS TO MYSELF.
VAMPIRE SNEEZE!
VAMPIRE SNEEZE!
"I WANT ANSWERS, OCTAVIUS!"

OSCORP.
NORMAN OSBORN'S HIGH-TECH EQUIPMENT COMPANY.
THIS NEW SPIDER-MAN 2 HAS MANY OF THE SAME QUALITIES AS OUR VENOM EXPERIMENT, ONLY MORE FOCUSED. MORE...
...DEADLY.
SO WHAT I WANT TO KNOW IS--
OSCORP
OSCORP

--WHO GOT THEIR HANDS ON MY PROPERTY, AND HOW DID HE MAKE BETTER MODIFICATIONS TO IT THAN THE SO-CALLED SCIENTIST TO WHOM I'M PAYING TOP DOLLAR?

REPAIR THE DRAGON MAN ANDROID AND SEND HIM OUT TO DO FURTHER TESTS.
I'LL CHECK BACK IN LATER.
DAD?

NOT NOW, HARRY, I'M IN THE MIDDLE OF SOMETHING IMPORTANT.
BUT, DAD, I HAVE SOMETHING UNBELIEVABLE TO TELL YOU!

UNLESS YOU WANT TO TELL ME YOU'VE FINALLY PULLED YOUR GRADES UP, THERE'S NOTHING YOU CAN SAY RIGHT NOW THAT I'D WANT TO HEAR.
AND I THOUGHT I TOLD YOU TO NOT DROP IN UNANNOUNCED ANYMORE.
NEXT TIME, CALL MS. HAND TO SCHEDULE AN APPOINTMENT.
I HAVE TO GO NOW.

I PROMISE YOU, DAD...

"...I'LL MAKE YOU NOTICE ME."
TRACKING SOMEONE ISN'T QUITE SO EASY WITH EIGHT POUNDS OF SNOT SMOTHERING MY SPIDER-SENSE...
...BUT I CAN'T STAY HOME KNOWING THAT VENOM HARRY IS OUT HERE SOMEWHERE!

WHOOPS!
SORRY TO GET IN YOUR WAY, FELLAS!

WITHOUT MY SPIDER-SENSE, I'M PRACTICALLY FLYING BLIND OVER--

SPAK!
OH.
HELLO.

SQUAWK!
NYAA!

OUT OF MY WAY, SPIDER-MAN
FTT

BRAKOOM!

HE'S MINE!
CRUNCH!
ALL RIGHT! IT'S SPIDER-MAN 2!
SAY "CHEESE"!

HISSSSSS!

HUH?
YEAH!
WAIT... WHAT--

UH-OH.
THAT'S MY CUE--

--SPIDER-MAN 1, CLEANUP IN AISLE FIVE!
WHOOSH
SNARE!

SHUNK SHUNK

HEY! YOU'RE SUPPOSED TO BE A GOOD GUY!
DON'T BE SUCH A PARTY POOPER, WEB-HEAD!

PUT THAT CAR DOWN, VENOM!

IF YOU INSIST!
HERE!
CATCH!

UNF!
VVVVSSSSSHHHHHH!

WHOA!
WHOA!
WHOA!
WHOA!

GOT IT!
ARE YOU OKAY, PAL?
A-OKAY, SPIDEY!

HAVEN'T YOU HEARD, SPIDER-MAN? YOU'VE BEEN REPLACED!
GO AWAY BEFORE I MAKE YOU GO AWAY!

AHH... THERE YOU ARE...

HOLD ON TO YOUR TONGUE! 'CAUSE HERE I COME!
FIGHT!

WHOOSH!
HA!

SPROING!
MISSED ME, MISSED ME, NOW YOU GOTTA KISS--

OKAY, *THAT* WAS CLOSE!
BOOM!

I CAN GET CLOSE TOO, YOU KNOW!

POW!
UNNN...

YOU HAVE TO GET ME OUT OF HERE, SPIDER-MAN!
HELP M--

GET BACK DOWN, OSBORN--
--THIS ISN'T YOUR FIGHT!
SLURP

EWWW!
DUDE, THAT'S YOUR TONGUE!
SPLORCH

ACK!
GERMS!
GERMS!

OSCORP
OH, NOT THE BUS! NOT THE BUS!
HONK HONK

SPLAT
‹PLEASE INSERT YOUR OWN BUG-ON-A-WINDSHIELD JOKE HERE.›

C'MERE! I'M NOT FINISHED WITH YOU YET!
I WAS AFRAID YOU'D SAY THAT.
THWIP

--AND THAT WALL-CRAWLING MENACE, SPIDER-MAN, IS NEXT!
CRASH

I'M GONNA SHOW YOU SOMETHING THAT'LL CHANGE YOUR LIFE!
DAILY BUGLE COMMUNICATIONS ISN'T JUST ABOUT BRINGING YOU THE NEWS...
HNNN...

I'M GONNA TEAR YOU LIMB FROM LIMB!

WE'RE ABOUT PROVIDING YOU WITH PRODUCTS THAT YOU NEED!
HOO BOY!

THINK FAST, PETER!
HEY, VENOM...

...I HOPE YOU'VE ALWAYS DREAMED ABOUT BEING ON THE BIG SCREEN--
WHAK!
FORGET BEDBUGS, IF YOU'VE GOT A WALL-CRAWLER ISSUE LIKE I DO...
...USE BUGLE BRAND INSECT SPRAY!
REMEMBER, FOLKS, J. JONAH JAMESON IS A MAN YOU CAN TRU--
BZZT!
BZZRRRRRKKKKTTT
--BECAUSE YOU'RE LITERALLY ON THE BIG SCREEN!

FOOM

YIKES! I WASN'T QUITE EXPECTING SO MUCH BANG FOR MY BUCK. WHAT ABOUT--

ZZZTT
HARRY!

DON'T WORRY, I GOT YOU!
WHUD

SP-SPIDER-MAN? WHAT HAPPENED?
YOU TELL ME.

THE SUIT...I THOUGHT I COULD CONTROL IT. BUT...I GUESS I ALMOST...LOST MYSELF.
DIDN'T I?

YOU WERE JUST A LITTLE BIT SICK, THAT'S ALL. IT HAPPENS.
I OWE YOU BIG TIME. I'M HARRY OSBORN, BY THE WAY.
HI, HARRY, I'M--AHH... AHH....

DUDE!
AH-CHOO!

VAMPIRE SNEEZE!
ALWAYS!
SORRY. SNF

WILL YOU BE OKAY?
POWER AND FAME ARE GREAT AND ALL....
...BUT VENOM? THAT'S NOT WHO I AM.
AND IF I HAVE TO BE SOMETHING OTHER THAN MYSELF TO GET MY FATHER'S APPROVAL...

...THEN I DON'T WANT IT.
CRUNCH
I DON'T KNOW ABOUT YOUR DAD, HARRY...

...BUT AFTER SEEING WHAT I JUST SAW...
...I BET YOU HAVE A BEST FRIEND SOMEWHERE OUT THERE WHO'D BE VERY PROUD OF YOU RIGHT NOW.
THE END

MARVEL UNIVERSE ULTIMATE SPIDER-MAN #19

OSCORP.
NEW YORK CITY.
DAD?
I--I NEED TO TALK TO YOU...
OSCORP
OSCORP
HARRY, I TOLD YOU NOT TO BOTHER ME AT WORK ANYMORE WITH YOUR HIGH SCHOOL DRAMA--
DAD!
DON'T BLOW ME OFF LIKE THAT! THIS IS SERIOUS!
WHATEVER IT IS WILL HAVE TO WAIT.
NO!

IT CAN'T!

THIS CAN'T WAIT!

H-HARRY?

ROOOAAARRR!

HARRY, IT DOESN'T HAVE TO BE THIS WAY.
THINK OF ALL WE CAN DO NOW...
...MY BOY!
THWAP!
MR. OSBORN, GET TO SAFETY!
I DON'T KNOW HOW LONG I CAN HOLD HIM BACK!
WHY WOULD YOU WANT TO HOLD HIM BACK?
YOW! GET OUT OF THE WAY, HE'S TOO STRONG!
RRRR!
CRASH!
YOU HAVE NO IDEA HOW LONG I'VE WAITED FOR YOU TO-- UHNN!
WAP!
NO!

AAAAAHHHHHHHHH!

GRAB!

THWIP!

PRETTY HEROIC STUFF, HUH?

MR. OSBORN--!
IT'S ALL RIGHT, I'M FINE.

VENOM TOOK OFF. H-HE'S GONE.
INDEED HE IS...

IN ANY CASE, YOU SAVED MY LIFE AND I'M VERY GRATEFUL. BUT I'D APPRECIATE IT IF YOU DIDN'T STALK AROUND MY BUILDING.
I HAPPENED TO BE SWINGING BY AND MY SPIDER-SENSE--
IF YOU'LL EXCUSE ME...

I HAVE BUSINESS TO ATTEND TO.
YOU CAN LEAVE THE SAME WAY YOU CAME IN.
I WON'T SEND YOU A BILL FOR THAT BROKEN WINDOW.

THAT'S WEIRD, RIGHT? IT'S NOT JUST ME?
I HAVEN'T SEEN MY BEST FRIEND HARRY OSBORN IN A WHILE, I WAS HOPING HIS VENOM DAYS WERE BEHIND HIM.
LOOKS LIKE IT'S TIME FOR ME TO GET TO WORK, TOO.
THE S.H.I.E.L.D. HELICARRIER.
OBVIOUSLY THERE'S ONLY ONE WAY TO HANDLE THIS...

WE HAVE TO DO WHATEVER IT TAKES TO TAKE VENOM DOWN RIGHT NOW.
NO OPTION IS OFF THE TABLE.
WE'LL TAKE HIM ON AS A TEAM.

IRON FIST IS RIGHT. JUST POINT US IN THE RIGHT DIRECTION, FURY. WE'LL BREAK HIM IN HALF!

AND WHEN POWER MAN'S DONE PUMMELING HIM, I'LL BLAST HIM INTO NEXT WEEK!

VENOM'S A SYMBIOTE MONSTER WHO BONDS TO A HOST. THAT MEANS THERE'S SOMEONE INSIDE OF IT.
YOU'RE JUST GONNA BLAST HIM TOO, NOVA?

"HIM," PARKER?
HOW DO YOU KNOW VENOM'S HOST IS A HIM?

I...
I CAN'T TELL YOU.
WHAT?

WHAT PART OF "TEAM" DO YOU NOT UNDERSTAND, WEB-HEAD?

YOU KNOW I'VE GOT A THING ABOUT PROTECTING SECRET IDENTITIES, WHITE TIGER.
EVEN FROM YOU GUYS.

THAT'S NOT THE RESPONSE I WAS LOOKING FOR.
FURY, LET ME HAVE ONE MORE CHANCE AT BRINGING HIM IN SOLO.
SORRY, KID, LIKE AVA SAID, WE'RE A TEAM--

--YOU EITHER GO IN AS A TEAM, OR YOU'RE OFF THE ASSIGNMENT ALTOGETHER.
...
FINE--

"--TOGETHER IT IS."
I'M GONNA BREAK YOUR SOULS INTO PIECES.
NICE FRIEND YOU GOT THERE, SPIDEY.

HE DOESN'T SOUND VERY FRIENDLY TO ME!

ZRAKK!
AAARGH!

WHOA! TAKE IT EASY, NOVA!
THWIP
THWIP

WHAT--?
THWAP!

WHAT IS YOUR DAMAGE? WE HAVE OUR ORDERS!
TAKE YOUR COSMIC POWERS DOWN A NOTCH. THERE'S SOMEONE INSIDE THAT THING.
WE CAN DO THIS SO NO ONE GETS HURT!

SAYS YOU, DORK.
WHOEVER'S IN THERE IS LONG GONE. HE'S ALL VENOM NOW.
IT'S TIME FOR MY S.H.I.E.L.D.-ISSUE TIGER CLAWS TO LEAVE THEIR MARK.
LET'S TAKE HIM, TEAM!

HNN!
ROOOAAARRRR!
KEEYAH!
WHOA!

ROOAAARRR!
SHUNK!

THUNK!
TEAM, I HAVE AN OPENING!

NO!
LET'S SEE IF HE'S ANY MATCH FOR MY IRON FIST!
POW!

AAARRRRPHH

WHERE DID HE GO?
UNDERGROUND?
HE GOT AWAY!
CRASHHH

I TOLD YOU THAT WASN'T THE WAY TO HANDLE THIS.
NOT ALL OF HIM GOT AWAY...

I GOT A SAMPLE.

OH.
THAT WAS ACTUALLY... BRILLIANT.
WHAT'S GOING ON HERE?

WHAT ARE YOU DOING IN MY LAB?
MR. OSBORN, WE'RE TRYING TO HELP.
I DON'T REMEMBER ASKING YOU FOR IT.

YOU NEED TO LEAVE RIGHT NOW...
...AND STAY OUT OF MY FAMILY'S AFFAIRS.

"FAMILY AFFAIRS"?
THAT MEANS...

"NORMAN OSBORN KNOWS VENOM'S SECRET IDENTITY, TOO."
OKAY, MAN, IT'S JUST US--
MIDTOWN HIGH.
AFTER HOURS.

--NO TEACHERS, NO DIRECTOR FURY--
NO WITNESSES.
WE ARE STANDING IN THE CIRCLE OF TRUST. IT'S TIME TO COME CLEAN.

YOU WERE ACTUALLY PROTECTING VENOM... FROM US. YOUR OWN TEAMMATES.
NO MORE GAMES. TELL US THE TRUTH. WHAT DO YOU KNOW?

WHEEL! OF! DECISIONS!
OKAY.
OKAY.
HERE'S THE THING--
--THE PERSON TRAPPED INSIDE OF VENOM IS...MY BEST FRIEND.
THE REAL ME, PETER PARKER'S BEST FRIEND.
HARRY OSBORN.
... OKAY.
YOUR MORAL DILEMMA MAKES SENSE NOW.
HOW DID THAT HAPPEN?

AT FIRST HARRY WAS HAVING FUN PLAYING SUPER HERO.
HE THOUGHT HE COULD CONTROL VENOM, BUT HE LOST IT. HE'S IN WAY OVER HIS HEAD.

SO HARRY'S TRAPPED INSIDE AND VENOM'S USING HIS BODY AS A HOST TO DO HIS DIRTY WORK?
WHAT ELSE DO YOU KNOW?
THAT'S ALL. I WISH I DID HAVE SOME CLUE AS TO HOW TO GET HARRY OUT.
YOU MEAN...

...A PIECE OF THE SYMBIOTE MONSTER?
LIKE THIS ONE?

RIGHT!
I'LL TAKE THIS TO THE CHEM LAB AND SEE IF I CAN WHIP SOMETHING UP. AN ANTI-VENOM!
YOU CAN DO THAT?

YOU DIDN'T FORGET THAT I'M A TOTAL SCIENCE NERD, DID YOU?

MOMENTS LATER...
OKAY, WHILE SPIDEY PLAYS PROFESSOR, IT'S UP TO US TO FIND VENOM.
EASIER SAID THAN DONE, POWER MAN--
HE COULD BE ANYWHERE IN THE CITY.
CRASH!

YOU TOOK A PIECE OF ME.
I WANT IT BACK.
WHEN HE PUTS IT LIKE THAT, WE SHOULD HAVE KNOWN THAT HE WOULD COME TO US.
I'M GOING TO EAT YOUR BRAINS!
REMEMBER, TEAM, WE DON'T WANT TO HURT HARRY, WE JUST WANT TO STOP VENOM!
HNN!

SOMEONE TELL HIM THAT!
ARGH!
YAAAAA!
AHH!
KROOOM!
STAY IN YOUR CORNER, BIG FELLA!
CRASH!
SMASH!
NO!
YOU STAY IN YOURS!
HNN!
HOW MUCH TIME DOES SPIDER-MAN NEED?

WATCH IT! HARMING MY BEST FRIEND IS NOT THE WAY TO MY GOOD SIDE, VENOM.

IT'LL TAKE MUCH MORE THAN THAT FOR HIM TO KEEP ME DOWN, IRON FIST.
LET'S SEE HOW MANY POUNDS OF PRESSURE IT TAKES TO DROP HIM, THOUGH--

CRUNCH!
HUNN!
GET OFF OF ME!

HE'S TOO STRONG!
NOVA!

UHN!
CLUDD!

WHERE IS SPIDER-MAN WITH THAT ANTI-VENOM?

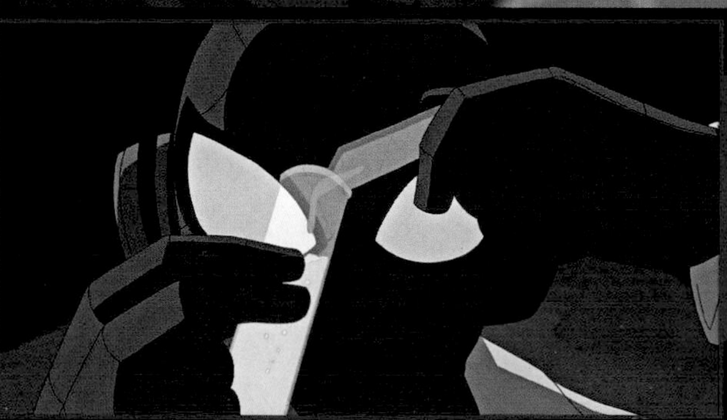

EUREKA! I'VE GOT IT!
YOU GUYS FIND HIM YET?
SSSSPIDER-MANNNN
I'LL TAKE THAT AS A YES.
HEY, VENOM, IF YOU WANT ME...
...THEN COME AND GET ME!
RRRAAAAAAAARR
KLANK!

YOINK!
DIE!
CRUNCH!
HARRY, I DON'T WANT TO FIGHT YOU, I WANT TO HELP YOU!
WHOOSH!
I KNOW YOU'RE STILL IN THERE!
WHOOSH!
PLEASE JUST--

ERRGH!
KA-POW!

THE ANTI-VENOM!
WHERE DID IT--?

I'M GONNA EAT YOUR BRAINS!

...YOU HAVE TO KNOCK IT OFF WITH THE EATING BRAINS THING.

KRAKOOM!

IT'S REALLY DISGUSTING.

HARRY! ARE YOU OKAY? CAN YOU GET FREE?

SPIDER-MAN, YOU HAVE TO HELP ME--
--YOU HAVE TO--

THERE IS NO HARRY!
THERE IS NO ONE ELSE!
THERE IS ONLY VENOM!
THEN I WON'T FEEL SO BAD--

POW!
--WHEN I DO THIS!
REMEMBER US?

THIS IS OUR CHANCE, TEAM! WE'LL KEEP VENOM BUSY...
...SO SPIDER-MAN CAN FINISH THE JOB.

THWAP!
ALREADY AHEAD OF YOU, POWER MAN!

HOW MANY TIMES DO I HAVE TO DEFEAT YOU--
--BEFORE YOU LEARN?
SORRY, VENOM--
--A TEAM AS TIGHT AS OURS--
--CAN BE PRETTY DARN STUBBORN!
GIDDYUP!
THUD
HUH?
LET'S SEE IF I'M AS BIG A SCIENCE NERD AS I CLAIM TO BE!
SHUNK!
RRROOOOOAAARRR!

WHAT DID--
--WHAT DID... YOU...
THUD
HARRY!
IS...IS VENOM GONE...?
YOU'RE SAFE, HARRY. YOU'RE WITH FRIENDS NOW.
IT'S OVER.

IT'S OVER.
"WE NEED TO TALK."

WE'RE IN THE MIDDLE OF A TRAINING SESSION, PARKER.

IT'LL ONLY TAKE A MINUTE, WHITE TIGER.
I JUST WANT TO APOLOGIZE FOR KEEPING SECRETS FROM YOU. IT WAS WRONG.
I WAS AFRAID THAT IF I GAVE UP VENOM'S IDENTITY, PEOPLE WOULDN'T LOOK AT HIM THE SAME AGAIN.

WE'RE YOUR FRIENDS, WEB-HEAD. HARRY'S, TOO.
YOU HAVE TO LEARN TO TRUST US, OKAY?

TRUST IS THE STRONGEST BOND.
THANKS FOR BEING SO UNDERSTANDING. AND THANKS FOR YOUR HELP--

--I COULDN'T HAVE BEATEN VENOM WITHOUT YOU.
OF COURSE I WAS THE ONE WHO CREATED THE ANTI-VENOM. YOU GUYS OBVIOUSLY WEREN'T GOING TO BEAT HIM WITHOUT IT.
...BUT OTHER THAN THAT...

YOU SMUG LITTLE--
HOLD IT, TIGER.
NOW THAT THE WHOLE TEAM IS HERE FOR A TRAINING SESSION, LET'S RUN THROUGH A NEW WORKOUT...

...CALLED "SQUASH THE SPIDER."
YIKES! WITH FRIENDS LIKE YOU, WHO NEEDS ENEMIES?!

THE END.